Snap books™

The World of Fashion

Fashion
HISTORY

Looking Great
Through the Ages

by Jen Jones

*Consultant: Kevin L. Jones
Costume Curator
The Fashion Institute of Design &
Merchandising Museum
Los Angeles, California*

Capstone
press®

Mankato, Minnesota

Snap Books are published by Capstone Press,
151 Good Counsel Drive, P.O. Box 669, Mankato, Minnesota 56002.
www.capstonepress.com

Library of Congress Cataloging-in-Publication Data
Jones, Jen.
   Fashion history: looking great through the ages / by Jen Jones.
   p. cm.—(Snap books. The world of fashion)
   Summary: "Explains the history of fashion as an industry and how the
styles have changed through the years"—Provided by publisher.
   Includes bibliographical references and index.
   ISBN-13: 978-0-7368-6828-0 (hardcover)
   ISBN-10: 0-7368-6828-3 (hardcover)
   ISBN-13: 978-0-7368-7882-1 (softcover pbk.)
   ISBN-10: 0-7368-7882-3 (softcover pbk.)
   1. Clothing trade—History—Juvenile literature. 2. Fashion—History—
Juvenile literature. I. Title. II. Series.
TT497.J66 2007
391.009—dc22   2006021848

Editor: Amber Bannerman
Designer: Juliette Peters
Photo Researcher: Charlene Deyle

Photo Credits:
Corbis/Bettmann, 11, 14, 27; Corbis/David Turnley, 20; Corbis/Kevin Fleming, 7; Corbis/Quadrillion, 13 (top); Corbis/
Reuters/Lucy Nicholson, 24; Corbis Sygma/Carraro Mauro, 21; Corbis Sygma/Sunset Boulevard, 19; Getty Images Inc./
American Stock, 15; Getty Images Inc./Chaloner Woods, cover (right), 16; Getty Images Inc./Fox Photos/George W. Hales,
13 (bottom); Getty Images Inc./Frank Driggs Collection/Frank Driggs, 12 (bottom); Getty Images Inc./Hulton Archive,
12 (top); Getty Images Inc./Stone/Robin Lynne Gibson, cover (left); Getty Images Inc./Stone+/Stephen Stickler, 5; Getty
Images Inc./Taxi/Eric O'Connell, 29; Getty Images Inc./Time Life Pictures/Pix Inc./Time Life Pictures, 17; The Granger
Collection, New York, 8, 9, 10, 23; Michele Torma Lee, 32; North Wind Picture Archives/North Wind, 25; Shutterstock/SI,
28; Shutterstock/Vanda Grigorovic, 18; Shutterstock/Wendy Perry, 6

1 2 3 4 5 6 12 11 10 09 08 07

Table of Contents

Common Threads

In 2003, a team of German professors made an interesting discovery. While studying human body lice, they decided that clothes were first worn about 40,000 years ago. How did they know? The type of lice dating back that far could only survive by laying eggs in fabric. Talk about hatching a trend!

This book brings you back in time to clothing's beginnings. We'll explore the history that makes fashion so fascinating. We'll also revisit the biggest trends throughout time, from leisure suits to leg warmers. Prepare to take a fantastic fashion voyage!

Chapter One

Traveling Through Time: The Journey from Function to Fashion

Most of us can't remember a time before our closets were full of cute clothes. Yet our early ancestors didn't have all the clothes that we do. Cavemen wore animal hides to fight the winter cold. In warm weather, they wore loincloths.

As time passed, new discoveries made it possible to create new fashions. Thousands of years ago, the Chinese created silk from the cocoons of silkworm moths. In 1792, Eli Whitney invented the cotton gin, which removed seeds from cotton. By hand, it took several hours to produce one pound of cotton. The cotton gin allowed workers to clean up to 50 pounds (23 kilograms) of cotton daily. Imagine all the cozy cotton clothing that could then be made! Today, silk and cotton are still used for many fashionable styles.

Cotton gin

Revelations of the Times

If you lived in Europe in the 1700s, you would have witnessed a time of great thought and social change. Historians call that time the "Age of Enlightenment." The machines of that era changed the way people earned a living. Many people left their jobs on the farm to become factory workers.

Singer sewing machine, 1851

Throughout the 1700s and 1800s, several breakthroughs paved the way for mass production of clothes. In 1733, John Kay invented the flying shuttle for the loom. This machine sped up the weaving process. Perhaps the most exciting invention was Edmund Cartwright's power loom. His loom used water as a power source. Made in 1785, it was the first loom to produce large amounts of cloth. Following in its footsteps were modern sewing machines. Elias Howe and Isaac Singer made these time-saving machines in the mid-1800s.

Pioneers of Fashion

Some of the world's greatest fashion pioneers created styles that are still "in" today. Thank Levi Strauss for your favorite blue jeans. During the California gold rush of the mid-1800s, Strauss created sturdy canvas pants for miners. The pants were instantly popular. Strauss later used heavy blue denim instead of canvas. An American tradition was born!

Employees outside of Levi Strauss & Co., 1880

Coco Chanel

Gutsy designer Gabrielle "Coco" Chanel was the brain behind groundbreaking fashions that set the modern stage. She believed fashion should be comfortable. In the 1920s, she popularized wardrobe staples like the wool jersey cardigan. What a welcome change for women who'd been holding their breath in corsets for years!

"Fashion changes; style remains."
– Coco Chanel

Time Machine

Charles Worth establishes the first haute couture fashion house in Paris. His pricey designs for royalty and wealthy American patrons set the tone for modern couture luxury.

To showcase the work of American designers, fashion publicist Eleanor Lambert organizes "Press Week." In later years, the event becomes New York's Fashion Week.

1857　　**1930s**　　**1943**

Smooth Harlem jazz musicians adopt zoot suits as their unofficial uniform. The zoot suits have padded shoulders and wide trousers.

Lady Diana Spencer marries Prince Charles in a lace and silk wedding gown with a 25-foot (8-meter) train. Afterward, millions of women around the world copy Princess Diana's sense of style.

1964   1981   2005

The clothing and textile industries trade is worth more than $400 billion globally.

Designer Andrés Courrèges introduces the "Space-Age" look just in time for the first moon landing. Other designers follow his lead. People everywhere strut their stuff wearing white and silver clothing made of vinyl and plastic.

13

Chapter Two

Icons and Period Pieces: Signs of the Times

The dawn of the 20th century was a time of romantic, flowing fashions. It was also a time of tailored outfits for the "new" active woman. Artist Charles Gibson drew the "ideal American woman." In his drawings, the "Gibson Girl" wore her hair piled high atop her head. She was shown out and about in high-collared dresses or in less restrictive, sporty clothing. Women following Gibson's style wore corsets around their waists to achieve the "S" curve of the look.

"Gibson Girls"

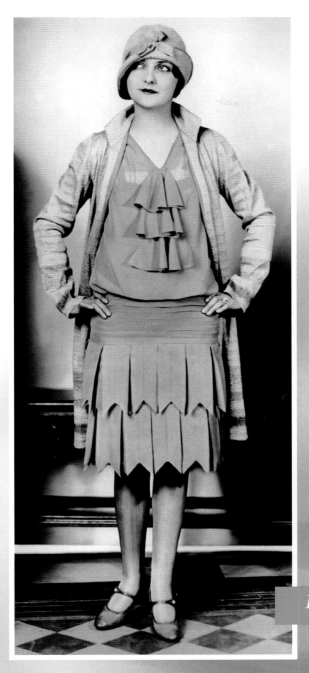

Flapper

When World War I began in 1914, the popular "Gibson Girl" look quickly went out of style. Men were away at war, so more women worked outside of the home. They shed their corsets for nursing uniforms and factory aprons.

During the 1920s, daring "flappers" took their fashion cues from Coco Chanel. She popularized the garçonne (or boyish) style. Today, the Roaring Twenties are known for those fiery, fabulous flappers!

Schoolgirl Chic: The '40s and '50s

In the late 1940s, designer Christian Dior introduced the "New Look." He designed long, full skirts with tight waistlines. This trend set off the feminine looks of the 1950s. Women swished about in full circle skirts or strutted around town in slim pencil skirts.

Pencil skirt

The poodle skirt was a popular fad in the '50s. Teens loved these colorful, felt skirts. Some had sewn-on poodle patches. They were all the rage at "sock hops," or high school dances, and socials. High school girls also wore their boyfriends' letter sweaters around town. What better way to bebop and cruise around in style?

Poodle skirt

17

Hippie Chicks and The Days of Disco: The '60s and '70s

The 1960s marked many turning points in history. The first man landed on the moon. Thousands of soldiers died in Vietnam. With political turmoil in the air, young people became peace-seeking "hippies." Hippies liked to go against the norm. They shopped for funky clothes like bell-bottomed pants with wide legs. The style of "bell-bottoms" was born!

Bell-bottoms were popular until the mid-1970s, when the disco days were in full swing. Thanks to the movie *Saturday Night Fever*, the polyester leisure suit worn by John Travolta became a notable fashion. Topped off by gold chains, these stylish suits were worn by dancing dudes everywhere!

*John Travolta in his
leisure suit*

You Glow, Girl: The '80s through Today

Tracing the trends of the '80s isn't hard to do. Almost all fashion fads were inspired by pop culture. For instance, the leg warmer craze came hot on the heels of the movie *Flashdance*. After pop sensation Madonna hit the scene, girls wore lace gloves and fishnet tights.

When not imitating the stars, '80s fashion was all about bold statements. Girls wore three colorful pairs of socks stacked over jeans. They wore brightly colored rubber bracelets. Shiny neon shirts, acid-washed jeans, and jelly shoes were the name of the game.

Madonna

The flamboyant fashion tide turned once the '90s were in full swing. Girls wore cutesy "baby doll dresses" and long-sleeved bodysuits. People also imitated their favorite "grunge" bands with flannel shirts and denim. Hip-hop style was also popular, with big, baggy jeans and suspenders.

Fashions are always evolving. Yet pieces of the past can be found in many new trends. The greatest part about fashion today is that anything goes. If you want to dress like a flapper or a flower-loving hippie, go for it! Chances are at some point that look will cycle back in style. Why not be a trendsetter?

Chapter Three

Through the Years: Clothing's Social Significance

Fashion reflects male and female roles in society. In the mid-1800s, it was common for men to work outside the home. Women commonly stayed home to raise children. When out in public, women wore uncomfortable hoop skirts and corsets. This was very different from the practical suits men wore.

Luckily for ladies, the strict rules of those days didn't last. By the turn of the 20th century, the "dress reform" movement came about. Women dared to wear shorter skirts. Yet these skirts were far from the miniskirts of today. They had lengths that weren't more than 5 inches (13 centimeters) off the ground.

Hoop skirt

Status and Fashion

Clothes say a lot about personality, self-image, and social status. Some people flash their wealth by wearing designer clothes or pricey accessories. At awards shows, celebrities parade down the red carpet in expensive designer clothing. The gowns and tuxedos are worth hundreds of thousands of dollars.

Actress Michelle Williams posing in dress by designer Vera Wang

Throughout history, society has put importance on fashion and wealth. Back in ancient Egypt, pharaohs wore headdresses and royal aprons to show rank. In 18th-century Scotland, members of high-profile clans wore bright multi-colored tartan, or plaid, clothing. Today, rock stars and movie stars set the fashion styles we all follow.

Ancient Egyptian queen (middle)

When describing fashion's influence—then and now—Mark Twain may have said it best: *"Naked people have little or no influence on society."*

Politics and Fashion

With so many worries during times of war, one might think that fashion would take a backseat. Yet during World War II (1939–1945), fashion played a surprisingly important role. Clothes were made with less material to save resources. For instance, men's pants no longer had cuffs. Women's skirts became shorter. With so many men off at war, women stepped into jobs formerly held by males. By 1945, women made up 36 percent of the workforce. Many women wore work pants, hairnets, and lace-up boots to protect themselves while working in manufacturing plants.

During the war, the Nazis kept the Americans and the British out of Paris. As a result, American and British designers and magazine editors couldn't go to France's fashion shows. New York and London then became important centers of the fashion world.

Factory worker, 1942

Society and Fashion

When it comes to the history of fashion, one thing is certain—clothes have always played an important role in society. That tradition is still very evident today. For example, clothing is used to show group belonging. Soldiers and police officers wear uniforms on duty. Sports teams dress the same to show unity and spirit. At some schools, students wear uniforms.

Clothing also impacts society in other ways. Certain kinds of clothes have stereotypes. A person wearing Birkenstock sandals might be labeled a hippie. A Ralph Lauren polo shirt may single someone out as preppy.

But no matter what a style might portray, remember that your clothes don't have to fit a mold to fit in. Take advantage of modern fashion freedoms. Do your own thing!

Glossary

ancestor (AN-sess-tur)—a family member who lived a long time ago

corset (KOR-set)—a fitted undergarment that was meant to give women a fashionable silhouette and support the bust

garçonne (gar-SON)—boyish style that was a fashion trend during the 1920s, popularized by Coco Chanel

haute couture (OHT koo-TUR)—high-end, one-of-a-kind fashion creations

waistline (WAYST-line)—the portion of the body between the lower ribcage and the pelvis bone

Fast Facts

In the late 1700s, Jacques Esnauts and Michael Rapilly created colored "fashion plates." These elaborate prints illustrated popular clothing styles. They were featured in *La Galerie Des Modes*, a fashion book of the time.

Barbie dolls were first introduced in 1959 at the New York Toy Fair. It was said that Barbie's career was fashion modeling.

The zipper was invented by Whitcomb Judson in 1893. Back then, it was called a "clasp-locker."

Read More

Gaines, Ann. *Coco Chanel.* Women in the Arts. Philadelphia: Chelsea House, 2004.

Hibbert, Clare. *A History of Fashion and Costume.* The Twentieth Century. New York: Facts on File, 2005.

Olson, Nathan. *Levi Strauss and Blue Jeans.* Graphic Library. Inventions and Discovery. Mankato, Minn.: Capstone Press, 2007.

Sills, Leslie. *From Rags to Riches: A History of Girls' Clothing in America.* New York: Holiday House, 2005.

Internet Sites

FactHound offers a safe, fun way to find Internet sites related to this book. All of the sites on FactHound have been researched by our staff.

Here's how:
1. Visit *www.facthound.com*
2. Choose your grade level.
3. Type in this book ID **0736868283** for age-appropriate sites. You may also browse subjects by clicking on letters, or by clicking on pictures and words.
4. Click on the **Fetch It** button.

FactHound will fetch the best sites for you!

About the Author

Jen Jones has always been fascinated by fashion—and the evidence can be found in her piles of magazines and overflowing closet! She is a Los Angeles-based writer who has published stories in magazines such as *American Cheerleader*, *Dance Spirit*, *Ohio Today*, and *Pilates Style*. She has also written for E! Online and PBS Kids. Jones has been a Web site producer for *The Jenny Jones Show*, *The Sharon Osbourne Show*, and *The Larry Elder Show*. She's also written books for young girls on cheerleading, knitting, figure skating, and gymnastics.

Index